LOUIS UNTERMEYER

The Second Christmas

*With Illustrations
by Louis Marak*

HALLMARK CARDS, INCORPORATED
KANSAS CITY, MISSOURI

Hallmark Cards, Inc. Kansas City, Missouri
THE SECOND CHRISTMAS
©1961 Louis Untermeyer. All rights reserved.
Library of Congress Catalog Card Number: 63-16482
Printed in the United States of America

A FOREWORD

What, I have been asked, are the authoritative sources of The Second Christmas. I am afraid that I cannot claim anything more "authoritative" than a friend's suggestion and an author's imagination. My friend, a very knowledgeable neighbor, and I had been discussing Biblical backgrounds, especially their relevance to past and present events. "Everyone knows what happened on the first Christmas," he said. "But what transpired on the second?" We became fascinated with the subject. He thought of an idea and I enlarged upon it; he indicated the outline of a narrative and I embroidered it; he presented a problem and I ventured to solve it. The story is the result.

Since it is the story of an escape — a kind of glorified suspense story — I considered calling it "The Refugees." But in the writing it took on the color and even the character of a legend. With the Bible as its inspiration I wove the customs of the period into something which was a cross between fact and fantasy. It was not until I had finished The Second Christmas that I suspected (or hoped) that I had created a legend that might have been true.

Newtown, Connecticut   Louis Untermeyer

5

THE SECOND CHRISTMAS

This is the legend they used to tell in the streets of Ghada more than a thousand years ago. Like every legend, it could have happened, and perhaps it did. Perhaps it was only a fragment of a greater tale remembered by the storytellers who came and went through the village. Erased by the blurring fingers of time, Ghada itself is now little more than a legend — pieces of a broken wall, parts of a ruined gate, scatterings of crudely cut stones are all that remain of the forgotten settlement at the edge of the desert. Ghada had never been built; it had merely accumulated, something that grew out of a junction, a crossroads where the caravan routes from the north and the east met, paused, and turned south into the limitless sands. No one thought of it as a town — towns were built for pleasure and permanence, with stout houses and bright shops and places of entertainment and a palace set in a park — but Ghada was a clutter of nondescript shelters raised on rocks and held together with rushes and caked mud. Those who lived there numbered fewer than two hundred.

The story begins before dusk of a certain day. It begins with a man leading a donkey, carrying a woman and a child. The woman was young and beautiful, and she held the child in her arms, for he was still a baby, and his face was covered with a veil against the blowing sand. The man was not old, but older than the woman; he was grizzled, heavy-set; the

tools of his trade hung from a rope knotted about his waist. The donkey was feeble and footsore. They had come a long way.

"Look," said the man, pointing toward the sunset, which colored the drab earth with transient loveliness. "Ghada. We can rest there."

It was farther than he thought. The weight of the air did not lessen; eddies of dust blew about them; the child whimpered; the donkey's hoofs slithered more and more uncertainly in the slipping sand. Twice the little beast fell to its knees, almost unseating its riders.

"It's tired," said the woman. "It's tired, poor thing — carrying me and the child."

"Only a little longer," said the man, as he helped the donkey to its feet and gently urged it on. "We will break our journey in Ghada. Perhaps the people will be kind. Perhaps we can stay a day or two before going on again."

"Perhaps," she repeated, shifting the child in her lap.

It was late dusk when they went through the Gate of the Camels. Lamps were being lit; camels grunted and bedded themselves down; groups of drivers stood about, gesturing, arguing, and exchanging gossip from the north and east; others squatted on the ground, holding spitted pieces of meat over small fires. Curious eyes followed the little group on its way across the dusty square, but no one spoke.

There was a well at the far end of the square. The man drew water while the woman got down, and some of the more inquisitive onlookers came closer.

"It's cooler now," said the woman. "He's sleeping."

First he offered the jar to the woman, then he drank, then he poured water for the donkey. It was not enough; the creature whinnied for more. The man drew another jar.

"Too much water is not good," said a voice at the man's elbow. "It will colic your donkey. I have seen camels die of drinking too much and too fast. Let your beast wait an hour — it is already bloated."

The man turned and saw a water carrier, barrel chested, swarthy, and

bearded, his empty waterskin hanging limply from one shoulder. The face was alive with an animal's cunning, the slyness of a fox hiding the savagery of a wolf. The body seemed sluggish, but the hands were quick as a trickster's, and the eyes were quicker.

"You come from the north," he said smoothly, "and you are running away. Oh, you need not deny it or ask me how I know. Even a drunken beggar dozing by the roadside could tell from your garb you are strangers and that you were too much in a hurry to change your heavy clothes. Then the donkey. Only a man fearing some sudden evil would risk his woman and her child on a half-dead creature unused to the sands. You could not wait to get a camel; you took the nearest — and the poorest — at hand."

Evading the water carrier's probing gaze, the man loosened the saddle and readjusted the packs. "Is there an inn here in the village?" he asked.

"An inn?" repeated the water carrier. "I suppose you could call it that. A lodging for camel drivers and traders and robbers. But—" he shook his head — "not for you, and surely not for a woman, with or without a child."

"Is there no other place?"

"No other."

"Then," said the man, with a worried look at the woman, who sat with drooping head at the well curb, "then we must go to the inn. We have come far, and we must rest — at least for this night."

"You will get no rest at the inn," said the water carrier glumly. "You would do better to lie down by the wayside and take your chances with the night prowlers."

"But with the child! No. We can go no farther. We will ask at the inn."

The water carrier filled his waterskin. "You cannot miss it," he said, and shrugged his shoulders, "but I will go with you."

The man turned the donkey toward the huddle of houses at the end of the road, and they moved on. They moved through silence. A few children pattered along after them, but there was no other sound. A potter, shaping the clay with his coaxing hands, lifted his eyes a moment from his bowl; a grain merchant, letting the seeds sift through his fingers, gazed idly at the passers-by; a mother with a child at her side stared from a doorway at the strange woman, whose look was so unlike her own. Then they came to the inn.

After the silence, the din was hideous. Shouting, cursing, and screaming burst from the place. The donkey refused to move.

"I told you you couldn't miss it," said the water carrier. "You can not

16

only see it but hear it — and smell it, too."

"What else is there for us?" said the man. "We must go on tomorrow. But tonight —"

"You will go on?" asked the water carrier. "Into the desert? The next stop is El Maresch, a long distance, and there are few wells between here and there. It is a difficult journey for a camel; for your donkey, it is impossible."

"We have no choice," said the man. "No choice for any of us."

"The desert is cruel," said the water carrier. "I have seen whole caravans depart from here and never come back. As for a helpless man with a dying donkey burdened with a woman and a child —" He looked at the woman. She said nothing, but he saw the sorrow in her eyes. "I am a poor man," the water carrier continued.

"I can pay," said the man. "I have

a little money for lodging and food for the animal. We do not require much."

"As I was saying," went on the water carrier, "I am a poor man. My house is small, and there are many children. But no one is so poor that he cannot share what little he has with someone who has less. For this night, the woman and her child shall rest. I cannot promise more. Come."

The place was a crowded hovel. Half-naked children cluttered the two rooms; chickens squawked, flying in and out; a goat, nursing its kid in a corner, kicked up its heels; and a lop-eared dog barked wildly as they entered.

"This," said the water carrier, "is where we live. These —" he made a sweeping, half-ironic gesture — "are my treasures, all of them. And this," he announced, as a woman round as a well-filled sack bulged into the room, "is my wife. This is Adira. My name is Akim. And you?"

"My name is — Jethro. And my wife is — Miriam."

"Well, let us see what we can do for the man who calls himself Jethro. My wife will look after the woman we will call Miriam. There is a little space left for those who are not too particular where they sleep."

It was just outside the house, little more than a lean-to, made of brush and wattles and clay. A door sagged on a broken hinge; there were no windows. It had once been a stable; moldy hay still lined the stalls, and the floor was covered with dried manure and bird droppings.

"Here!" cried Adira, bustling in and brushing off a hen roosting on a rack. "Out with you! Open the door; let in the air. A rat couldn't breathe here — let alone a child."

"It's not exactly a king's palace,"

grimaced Akim. "But it can be cleaned — there's fresh straw somewhere — and we can make a sort of bed for the woman and the child."

"I do not know how to thank you or even what to say," murmured Jethro.

"Say nothing, for it is nothing. Nothing but a brief shelter. But it will keep out the worst of the wind at night and the glare of the sun by day. And," he added slyly, "you will be well hidden."

"We are grateful," said the man Jethro, "both of us — all three of us," he continued, as the woman held up the child with a smile of relief. "But we will not be a burden for long. To-night we stay, but we must be on our way early in the morning."

"Let us talk about tomorrow to-morrow. First you must eat. 'He who's not fed can't rest in bed' is one of our oldest proverbs. Dothan!" he cried,

and a loose-limbed, black-eyed boy of fourteen pushed aside the door behind which he had been lurking. "Dothan is my oldest and laziest and least dependable son, but his broom knows how to be busy. Get it, Dothan. Stop grinning, and let it make you do what is to be done — quickly. And now," Akim resumed, "let us see what the insatiable mouths of my children may have left."

There were a bowl of lentils and onions, bits of lamb that had been skewered over wood embers, and coarse bread, warm from the clay oven.

Then Adira brought in a small flask. "Not for you," she said to the men, as she placed the milk before Miriam. And the two women smiled at each other.

They did not leave the next morning. The donkey seemed lame and was barely able to carry its own weight.

Nor did they depart the day following, for the strain on the mother had been great, and she was near exhaustion. A week later, they were still there. This time, the mother pleaded for further delay. "The child is sleeping so much better here, and my milk is better for the baby now. The people are generous; the children adore the baby. Let us stay a little longer."

So the days went by. Then the weeks. Then the months. The fear never left them, but they were no longer alone. There were women with whom a mother could share the glory of her child, women who understood the mystery of his motions, the waving little hands, even the occasional fretfulness — women who could feel the wonder of his growth, the very miracle of his being. And there were men with whom a man could converse — the endless but ever-fascinating talk of the day, the intricate details of a

cunning trade, the real reasons for an unreasonable quarrel, the guarded secrets of a skilled craft, the grain of truth in a bushel of lies, the lessons to be learned from fools and scoundrels. And there was always the pos-

sibility of news — or a sign. Their
lives, especially the woman's, had
been marked by signs. They were
waiting now, waiting for a sign that
would tell them whether they could
return — or whether they would have

to go on farther — and farther.

They said nothing to Akim; but he watched their questioning eyes whenever strangers came to the village. Akim was helpful. If he seemed half wolf and half fox, he was also part ferret. He could nose out news before it was told. Whenever a great caravan came through Ghada or a straggle of drivers stopped off at the well, Akim was there, manipulating some dubious transaction, handling oddments of merchandise gotten who knows where, haggling or haranguing, advising, expostulating, and agonizing, but always obtaining the last fragment of information concerning the outside world.

"A dull day, Jethro," he would say, pretending to ignore the man's anxiety. "Always the same. Thirst for gossip and thirst for water. Camel drivers are like their camels. They drink and make unlovely sounds with their bellies; they say nothing worth saying and know nothing worth knowing. I have time, and so I listen to them; but I never hear what I am listening for." Which was as much as he would tell Jethro, and Jethro never would ask him what he most needed to know.

It was the man's craft that broke the last barrier between them. He could not be idle during the months of waiting. He had sharpened his ax, polished the plane, refastened the head of his hammer, checked his measures, and put together a broken chisel. He found nails and pieces of wood; he made pegs and cut long boards. He began by repairing a neighbor's door. Then he put up shelves for the grain merchant. After he built a stand for the potter, he made stools and benches for growing families. Soon he was at work every day. The fear never left him; but it

28

was in the back of his mind, instead of in the forefront of his thoughts. He was often heard singing.

One evening, he placed a table of cedarwood against the wall. "That's a fine-looking article," said Akim, running his hand appreciatively over the surface. "Smooth as a woman's flesh — fashioned and molded with love. You did not learn to shape a thing like this overnight, nor in the time you've been here. Why you have hidden it, I cannot guess; but even a blind man feeling the shaping of this wood could tell that you are a carpenter and have always been a carpenter. Am I right?"

"You are not wrong. The chisel and the hammer and the ax are my fingers. I am nothing without them. But —"

"But there are things you could not tell me. I know," said Akim. "I also know there is a time when they should be told. I think the time has come — a time for trust."

"I shall tell you what I can," said the carpenter, and the relief was in his face as well as in his voice. "As you have guessed, we come from Judaea. The child was born in Bethlehem. My wife had visions long before that, and at the time of the child's birth, the air was full of portents. A great new star had suddenly appeared in the sky, and many had been guided to the manger where the child lay. Shepherds had come, and wanderers, and even — it is hard to believe — three kings from the East, who brought gifts for the infant. Strange gifts they were: gold, they said, for the glory the infant would attain; frankincense for the holiness that would surround him; bitter myrrh for the suffering he would undergo. We understood nothing of this; but word of these happenings got about, and rumors spread through Judaea. They reached the ears of King Herod, and he called together his priests, his scribes, and his soothsayers. After they had consulted for a long time — for they feared his wrath — they uttered a prophecy. They told Herod that the little town of Bethlehem would be not the least among the princes, for out of it there would come a governor who would rule the people, a true king of the Jews. When Herod heard that a rival king might have been born in his domain, he resolved to safeguard his throne by the most terrible means. Not knowing what child might be responsible for the threat, he gave orders that all the children two years old and under in Bethlehem and, to make certain, all along the coast, should be killed."

"But how did you learn of the decree in time?" asked Akim.

"It was a sign," said the carpenter.

"I had a dream in which a spirit appeared and told me that unless I took the child and his mother at once and set out for Egypt, we would be destroyed. Herod's messengers would either find us where we were or seek us out and kill the child."

"And so you hid. And so you have become one of us and yet not one of us. Safe though you are, you still do not know whether to go or to stay. It is as if you were waiting for something that would never come."

"It will come," said the man. "For good or bad, it will come."

"And what will it be?" pursued Akim.

"Another sign," said the carpenter, and took up his adze.

The women had split the stems of the flax; they had carefully combed the thin but useful strands; distaff and spindle had separated the finer threads to be woven into cloth. And now, swaddling the infant in soft linen, the mother crooned serenely and looked out across the earth. She, too, was waiting for a sign; but she waited without anxiety. A quiet day was drawing to a hushful close, and except for the sleeping child, she was alone.

It was on such a day and in such an hour that the first sign had come. It was back in Galilee, in the city called Nazareth. The room had seemed stiller than usual, almost too still. She knew that if she held her breath, she would hear the silence. It was as if the silence wanted her to listen. Then it spoke. It spoke with a rustling of wings and a flashing of light too brilliant to bear. When she opened her eyes, she saw the presence in the room, and a voice, like crystal speaking, turned the silence into sound.

"Hail," said the angel, "hail, fa-

34

vored of women. Blessed art thou, for the Lord is with thee."

The girl was frightened. She was a virgin espoused to a man of the house of David, and she was troubled at the salutation, uncertain of what it might mean.

The angel reassured her. "Fear not," he said. "Thou hast found favor with God, and thou shalt conceive and bring forth a son. And he shall be great and shall be called the Son of the Highest, and the Lord God shall give unto him the throne of his father David. And of his kingdom there shall be no end."

"But," she said, without lifting her eyes from the ground, "how can that be?"

She could not remember everything the angel had said; even then, she had not understood all of it. But his presence was promise and assurance, and she ceased to trouble about the meaning of the words. Holiness surrounded her while he spoke of the holy things of the spirit; fear departed, and comfort filled her heart as he told her that with God nothing is impossible. Then the wings swept by her, the light dimmed, and she was again alone.

And now here was the child, sleeping safely in the cradle his carpenter-father had made. Here was everything a mother could desire or dream of — everything except a home. Home. This, too, was a dream. All her life she had lived in a world of dreams, another world. Half dreaming, she yearned back to the land of her girlhood. She saw herself, as a child, holding the hand of another child at the Feast of Unleavened Bread; she watched herself grow taller and join the singers at the Celebration of the Blossoms and the First Fruits of the Field; she became a young woman and helped decorate the booths with grapes and pomegranates at the Festival of the Harvest; she played the part of the loyal and devoted Ruth at the time of the Reaping of the Corn.

The memories surged over her. Family preparations for the Passover. The smell of dill and cumin and other herbs drying in the hot sun. A visit to her cousin Elizabeth, who was bearing a child. Home.

It was late when her husband found her sitting in the dark. He studied her face as she lit the lamp. "You have been weeping," he said. She smiled sadly. "It is hard for you. Your thoughts are far away. You are lonely. You would like to return."

"You know. How?"

"How could anyone fail to know? When we first came here, you said nothing. You were glad to have escaped. Then, when the terror seemed far away and the fear grew less, you spoke of the future and planned for

38

the months ahead. But lately — when they gather the grapes grown heavy from the rain or go out to glean the ears of corn — your thoughts turn back. You never complain. You never let me see that there may be tears in your eyes. But you cannot prevent my noticing the way you talk."

"What way do I talk?" she asked.

"You no longer say, 'Let us do this,' or, 'Tomorrow we should do that.' Instead, you say, 'Let us do this after we return,' or, 'When we get home, we will do that.'"

"You are a good man —" she nodded — "and you know my mind. Tell me, then, when *will* we return?"

"I do not know," he sighed. "But when the time comes, when the sign appears, we will both know."

It must come soon, he thought. There had been no news for them from any source. Many caravans had come and gone; but there was no sign, no tidings to bring him back or drive him on. He was no longer afraid to go about the streets and mingle with the others in the square of the camel drivers. No one could recognize the harried refugee in the browned and bearded villager. Sometimes he went with Akim; sometimes he went alone; usually, however, he stayed at his bench and waited until Akim had gathered the last grain of gossip from the chafferers.

One day, when the child was almost a year old, he looked up from the heavy piece of algumwood he had been planing and realized Akim was in the room. Akim had been sitting silently for some time.

Finally, Akim spoke. "It may mean nothing," he said, "nothing at all. But there were strange men in the caravan today. It was a long, strange caravan, too — first, twenty camels; then, an hour later, twenty more; and in the third hour, another twenty. The square was so crowded they had to find places outside."

"I must see that sight," said the man who called himself Jethro.

"It would be better if you stayed away until —"

"Until when? Why?"

"Until I am sure. I do not know why — not yet — but one of the strangers, a tall man, has been asking questions. I came late, and he had disappeared. He got no satisfaction from anyone. If he is here tomorrow, I will find out more — enough, I hope, to help you — or to warn you."

That evening, the man and the woman, carrying the child, crept cautiously up the low hill that overlooked the whole of Ghada. There was a sunset, but not a quiet-colored one. The air was somber. There was no promise of peace in it. The clouds were jagged; the sky was a menacing red; a cold wind whipped against them. He knew she had been weeping.

She drew her shawl closer about her. "We cannot stay here," she said.

"Here?" he gestured. "On this hill? Or in Ghada?"

She did not answer for a moment. Then she said, "He was born on the seventh day of the new moon. That was almost a year ago. Is he to grow up among strangers? Will he never know his own people? Must we go on again?"

She, too, he thought, had heard something, a rumor, a threat that carried an echo of the old fear. This time, she could not conceal the tears.

"Where," she cried softly, "where will we be on his second birthday?"

He put his arm around her shoulders and kissed her forehead. "I will tell you tomorrow," he said.

The next day, Akim was certain. "I saw the tall stranger," he said. "He

was there again. A stranger he is; his
clothes, his bearing, and his speech
are those of another country. He
asked many questions of the villagers,
and when they shook their heads and
pointed at me, he came over to where
I was sitting at the well curb. His
manners were fine and his questions
smooth. At first, they were general —
far too general. How old was Ghada?
About how many inhabitants were in
the village? Had I lived here all my
life? Did I always meet the caravans,

and did I know anything of the out-side world? When I answered his easy questions, he became more definite. He wanted to know particularly about newcomers. Could I tell him about any odd-looking travelers who may have come through during the last year? I invented a few, but he pressed me further. Did I remember a heavy-set man whose hair showed streaks of gray and who carried a bag of tools, a man accompanied by a young woman carrying a babe on a donkey? I said I thought I recalled such a wandering family. They came alone, all alone? Yes, I nodded. When had they come? Many months ago, I replied. And were they still here? Oh, no, said I. They stayed only briefly. Where, then, did they go? On into the desert beyond the hills. Into the desert? he repeated. But they could not survive there. Probably not, I shrugged. But are you sure? he persisted. I shrugged again and moved off."

"What did he look like?" asked the carpenter.

"Like someone connected with a royal house. An officer, most likely — a king's officer. This is what you feared, is it not? Well, you need fear no more. He said he must continue the search — and I have watched the caravan making ready to depart."

That night, there was happiness in the little house at the edge of the town of Ghada. The carpenter told his wife that the threatening shadow had come and gone, that they need hide no longer. She ran to tell the good news to Adira, who rejoiced with her.

"We must celebrate," Adira shouted, clapping her hands and calling to her husband. "We must tell the people. People will come and share these good folks' joy. Let us not wait, but celebrate tomorrow."

"Wonderful," responded Akim.

"Wonderful, indeed," said the carpenter, "for tomorrow is the child's birthday."

It was a small celebration, but it was a loving one. The plain table in Akim's house had been brightened with many-colored leaves and sprays of almond blossoms. A neighbor had brought a jar of honey; another had arranged a bowl of melons and apricots; Dothan had picked a basketful of brambleberries. There were nuts and dates and pickled beans and flat cakes flavored with a sprinkling of coriander seeds. Akim had managed to exchange a piece of questionable information for a flask of palm-tree wine, and Adira had strewn the floor with mint and camphire, so that the fragrance scented the room at every footfall.

There were much going and coming, endless gossip, and gaiety.

Healths were drunk and long life pledged with every mouthful. There were sudden bursts of song, wanderers' chants and remembrances of ancient tunes. And, increasing the high spirits, there was dancing. None of the musicians could claim to be a performer; but one knew how to play the double-reeded shawm, another plucked the strings of a battered psaltery, a third made shrill sounds through a homemade flute, while a fourth struck a metal triangle and kept time with a wood-and-goatskin drum. The child slept through it all.

It was at the height of merrymaking that a tall shadow appeared in the doorway. There was no mistaking it. It was the officer who had asked the questions, had gone away unsatisfied, and had returned. The music stopped. The dancers drifted apart.

The room was tense with silence.

The figure advanced to where the carpenter was standing. "It took me a long time to catch up with you," he said. "An unnamed street at the end of an unlikely town. You were well hidden. But uncover you I did. You are known here as Jethro, but you are Joseph, the carpenter of Nazareth. And your wife, she who is sometimes called Miriam, is Mary. And there is your child. It has been a long search. But we were sworn to find you."

For a blank moment, no one moved. The horror in the room was tangible; the overheated air held daggers of ice. Then Akim's hand slid silently behind him. He picked up a knife and balanced it in his hand, ready for a quick thrust. Joseph, whose face had suddenly grown haggard, stepped in front of the niche in which the child was sleeping.

The officer flung up one hand and

called into the darkness. At his command, two figures came out of the night, pushing their way into the crowded room. The people shrank against the walls.

Mary, who had stood motionless, cried out, darted to the niche, and snatched up her baby. She stood quivering, her face dead white, half desperate, half defiant.

The officer pointed to the child, and the two men advanced. Joseph lunged toward the men. Before he could take hold of either of them, they dropped on their knees before Mary. Each one placed a box upon the floor.

The breathless moment eased into a sigh of amazement. Joseph drew himself erect, his hands hanging open and empty. Mary's arms relaxed their frightened clasp; her eyes dropped to the two bowed heads before her and then to the boxes so unexpectedly

at her feet.

They were sandalwood boxes, carved in high relief, tinted with many colors, and embellished with gold.

"They are for the child," the officer said into the hush. He bent down and opened the right-hand box. "Here is raiment, the purest textures the East can produce." He opened the left-hand box. "Here," he said, "is a crown of gold for a blessed head."

"The sign," breathed Mary.

"But who are you?" asked Joseph incredulously. "Why are you here?"

"To do the bidding of Melchior, whose name means King of Light."

"Melchior?" repeated Joseph.

"Do you not remember? It was he who, a year ago, with King Gaspar and King Balthasar, the other Kings of the East, followed a star to a certain manger. Do you remember now? And do you not also remember that gifts were brought then — gold and frankincense and myrrh?"

"Yes, yes, I remember," said Joseph. "But why these gifts — now?"

"To celebrate the beginning of a new world for us, a world of peace and love. It is a year now since King Melchior beheld something which he did not understand but which he came to believe. He had always gloried in power, in conflict and wars of conquest. Suddenly, on that night, something was revealed which was the opposite of hatred and war, something he saw reflected in the eyes of the shepherds, even in the eyes of the kneeling beasts. When he returned to his kingdom, everything in him had changed. Today, his country is no longer an armed camp but a place of peace. Melchior is not only a king but a Magus, a truly Wise Man. He could not forget the birthday of this child."

Joseph looked at Mary. Her eyes were clear with restored content.

"So they were not from Herod," Joseph murmured to her.

The officer caught the name. "Herod?" he said. "But Herod is dead. Herod is long dead, and his edicts have died with him. Word has not reached you yet?"

"No," said Joseph in bewilderment. "We never heard."

"There is one more gift from King Melchior," continued the officer.

"For you. A pair of camels to take you wherever you wish to go."

"Home," Mary whispered. "Home." She looked at Joseph and then at the child. He smiled up at her, and a radiance, an ever-growing glory filled the room.

Christmas Shelf

Untermeyer, Louis
The second Christmas.